"Sunni Dayz"

Written by
D C Bryant

Synopsis

Sunni Patterson, a smart, sexy, accomplished, young woman embarks on a well-deserved cruise with her beautiful best friend Brianna. Party shoes are must-have along with strength and resilience as Sunni and Brianna travel on their dream Western Caribbean vacation. It will take them places that they could not possibly imagine!

The Cruise

Sunni Patterson punched angrily at the boxing bag envisioning her ex-boyfriend's face. She had loved him so much...they had been through a lot together. Sunni, Brianna and Mark were inseparable since junior high. Mark and Brianna were at the hospital and held her down when her father died. Sunni's mom was never the same after her father's death.

So Sunni was glad she had her friends to lean on. She thought they would always be there for each other. Even, when Sunni earned a full scholarship to college,

Her friends followed her to Florida State.

Brianna was graduating with a

Communications degree. She always thought

she was a star and wanted to be on

television. Mark was a football phenom. He

was being scouted by major ball clubs but

that was no reason to let that shit go to his

head. In their senior year, bitches were

getting ridiculous. Chicks would openly flirt

with Mark right in front of her face. Sunni

tried not to let it bother her though. She

thought her relationship with Mark was

tight. Hell, if it were not for her tutoring

his sorry ass, he would not have the grades

to stay on the team.

How quickly he forgets, Sunni thought as

she hit the punching bag so hard, it seems to

reverberate forever. Sunni could not

believe that she walked into Mark's bedroom

and he was cock deep into some scank's ass.

She wasn't gonna cry even though it hurt like

hell. Sunni continued to punch and kicked

the bag as sweat pour down her perfectly

formed brown body. As she brushed back

the braids that fell loose, she thought of

the rough road to graduation. She would be

going to graduate school with a master's in

biology.

Sunni was tired and needed a break. She

still couldn't believe Mark. How could he

cheat on her! A knot grew in her throat as

tears rolled down her face.... Sunni was no

stranger to pain. While she developed into a

beautiful, young woman, she wasn't

always that way. Haters had bullied her

growing up. Yeah, she was a little skinny and

didn't have the trendy clothes. But Brianna

had come to her rescue anyway when the

popular girls teased her. Nobody fucked

with Brianna because they wanted to be her.

She was the pretty blonde next door that all

the guys wanted to hook up with. They

became fast friends. Brianna could charm

her way out of situations while Sunni

knowing that she was cute would use brains

or brawn! She left the superficial shit to

Brianna. Sunni began kick boxing not only

for protection but it helped to deal

with her frustrations.

It was hard losing her dad and watching her

mom go into a shell.

Sunni was glad she and Brianna were taking a

western cruise to Cozumel. They would sail

from Key West to Mexico and back. Sunni

was going to surprise Mark with a

ticket but he fucked up. The ship

disembarked the afternoon and Sunni

couldn't wait to get out of town for a while.

She called Brianna the next day to see if

she wanted to share a cab. The phone rang

and rang. Sunni texted her and finally got a

response. "Brianna, what the hell?" Sunni

texted! We only have hour! U ready 2 go?

Brianna texted. "Started the party las nite!

I'm packed, meet U @ the ship!" Sunni was a

little disappointed as she

hailed a cab on the way to the party ship.

Come on Brianna Sunni thought as she

glanced at her watch. The ships horn blew

as it began to disembark. Sunni's eyes

scanned the crowds of people cheering as

the ship drifted from the shore. Suddenly

she heard a sassy voice, "Hey, Diva looking

for me?" Brianna said. "Damn, Bri! You gotta

play it close to the vest, don't you?" They

began to laugh because it really wasn't that

serious.

Brianna asked Sunni about Mark as they ate

dinner. Sunni explained how she walked in on

Mark having sex with another woman.

Brianna tried to console Sunni realizing how close they had been. "You, know his fame has gone to his head. Just because he is about to be picked up by the NFL, he is seriously trippin!" Brianna assured her. "You are smart, beautiful and if he is too stupid to see that, well FUCK HIM! Mark is my friend too, but he hurt you and you deserve better. We are going to forget Mark and have some fun on this cruise, okay? Sunnnni!" Brianna suggested …. reluctantly Sunni agreed. The two women decided to explore the ship. The ship accommodates guests with decks of fun filled excitement.

The ship had three pools, casinos, several restaurants, shopping boutiques, gyms, salons, bars and nightclubs. "Look at that waterslide, Bri! You can glide down that bitch! Sunni taunted. "Oh, I see plenty I wanna go down on", Brianna joked as a handsome officer walked by. "Damn, girl that's the captain", Sunni whispered. "Hello, ladies. I am Captain Woods. I see you're admiring my vessel. Care for a tour of the bridge?" he asked.

"Sure!" The ladies replied in unison. Captain Woods introduced the women to first mate Johnson one of his crewmembers helping to steer the ship. Johnson smiled and continue to man the helm.

"This is where it all happens. Quite a view, huh? I control and command the entire ship from right here on the bridge. That includes the boiler, all onboard machinery and ship's navigation" the captain said as he grabbed the other wheel. The women smiled at each other. It seems the captain's grand gesture was more geared towards impressing them. "Captain so, you control everything from the bridge. Do you sleep here as well?" Sunni asked as her eyes curiously scanned the bridge. Her scientific curiosity kicked in as she walked toward a closed door and started to peek in. The captain abruptly said "I'm sure you ladies will enjoy your trip but looks like we are quickly approaching some rough seas. We will be reaching Cozumel in about two days. You remember how to get back to your quarters?" He asked. "Yes, sure and thanks for the tour", Sunni replied. The captain smiled at his first mate and commented, "Interesting" as the women left the bridge.

That was weird Sunni and Brianna agreed as they left. The women decided to chill out and get relaxing massages. Brianna took a selfie of them as they went to get on the massage tables. She snapped photos of the handsome masseurs, admiring their physiques.

They booked the massage room together to

chat while a hunky Francois and Miguel

slowly worked them over. Francois worked

deliberately to soothe Sunni's hard

working feet. His strong hands manipulated

her toes and moved into every pressure

point in Sunni's feet. She moaned

involuntarily as Francois worked up her

muscular but soft calves. As Francois

worked his hands up Sunni's firm but

soar thighs, she could not help but let out an

"Uhmmm!" that made Brianna giggle like a

schoolgirl. She told Sunni as a face limply

lay in the face hold. "This is heaven!"

Brianna said. "

I know, right!" Sunni agreed in a totally

relaxed tone. Francois traced Sunni's supple

thighs to her soft buttocks, she jumped

"Hey, hold up! Uh, my back is really sore,

okay?" Qui, mademoiselle, Francois said as

he reluctantly began to work every muscle in

her back. Miguel trying to please Brianna

asked, "Mi gustas, senorita? She replied,

"Oh yeah, I like" Brianna moaned as Miguel

slowly massaged every part of her body.

There were no boundaries to the pleasure he

gave to Brianna. Sunni laughed and said "Girl

you are so bad!" "Hey, you only live once",

Brianna replied. They left the sexy

masseurs, excited and ready for more fun.

The women were planning to go clubbing

and decided to change into some sexy

outfits. Brianna decided to buy a new outfit

from the Designer Boutique. She wanted

Sunni to come with her to pick out

something hot. After trying on several

dresses, Brianna bought two dresses. One

was a totally hot Jean P Gaultier flirty short

sleeve, pink, tunic lace mini and the other

was a yellow rhinestone encrusted,

sweetheart neckline with sequin bust, a-line

tulle short dress. They both

complimented her long legs. "Are you going

to get anything?" Brianna asked Sunni. "No,

I brought plenty outfits to choose from.

Besides, you are the money bags,"

 Sunni replied. Brianna had come from a well

to do but dysfunctional family. That was

why she was closer to Sunni than her own

family. "You can afford to buy something

new.

Just cash in the ticket you brought for

Mark! Oh Shit! That was insensitive of

me. I'm so sorry". Brianna apologized when

she saw the sad look on Sunni's face.

"Have you talked to him since we left?"

Brianna asked. "No, I don't fucking plan to

either no matter how many times he texts

me!" Sunni angrily

replied. "Can I help you?" The salesperson

asked forcefully. "Yes, you may", Brianna

said as she rolled her eyes and toss her

selection on the counter. She paid for her

purchase with her credit card and they

quickly left the store. Sunni jokingly

commented, "Brianna, you are such a bitch

sometimes!" "Whaaaat?" Brianna chuckled

as they made their way back to their cabins.

Sunni was dressed before Brianna in a clingy

white, channel dress with spaghetti straps

and 4 -inch Jimmy Chooz criss-cross, sandals

that really set off the ensemble. She

looked stunning and drew attention from

passersby as she stood in the moonlight

gazing at the water. The moonlight danced

on the waves that trailed the ship. Sunni

stared at the water but was deep in thought.

Her mind flashed back to her dad laying on

his deathbed. He was a cop and had been

shot in the line of duty. Her father had

taught her so much. He taught her how to

change a tire, to shoot a gun and especially

not to be afraid of life's experiences.

Her mom had told her that her dad wasn't

going to make it, but it was surreal. Sunni

peered at him threw teary eyes in disbelief.

"Daddy, you can make it, please don't leave

me! Please, please don't leave me and mom!

I'll be better! Daddy! I got an A on my

science project and the teacher said that

she was gonna see if I could get into

the advanced class." Sunni continued to

babble until the sound of the life support

machine made this disturbing sound that

made her scream for her mom. Her mom and

the nurse ran into the room but it was too

late, her dad was gone. Sunni and her

mom held each other for dear life. It seems

like the last time her mother ever really

held her that way again. It's funny how shit

changes Sunni thought. Their family

closeness was her rock and she would miss

how dad called her his Sunni day. She

recalled as she stared into the water, how

her dad taught her to swim. Once, she

caught on it was no stopping her. Sunni

could swim circles around her dad and any

boy in school for that matter. Sunni

reminisced wishing that time could got back

to the good days. Now, her mom was living in assisted living. The man she loved was a narcissistic whore. Sunni felt alone but knew she would have to keep it moving. As she stared at the water, Brianna's voice brought her back as she heard Brianna asking if she was ready to hit the club. "Sunni! Snap out of it. Come on sweetie. Let's go get faded," Brianna insisted. The club was popping. The women sauntered to the bar for drinks.

It was on, the music was slamming, and the crowd was jamming. They began with tequila and beer chasers and the party was on.

Partygoers were drinking, laughing, and dancing to the rhythmic, hypnotic music. Sunni and Brianna joined them on the dance floor. They shook their hips and moved their bodies seductively as amorous eyes watched. Sunni decided to get another drink to soothe her parched throat. As she ordered from the bartender, a stranger moved close. "You all in that dress baby, can I help you get out of it?" he slurred the lame come on.

The stranger moved in closer and accidently spilled her drink on her dress. "Oh shit! You just fucked up my dress!" Sunni shouted.

She quickly turned to find a bathroom. She was going to holla at Brianna, but she was hugged up with some hottie on the dance floor. So, Sunni found a bathroom and incessantly scrubbed the stain. It was pointless, the stain was not coming out. Sunni text Bri to let her know that she was going to the cabin to change. Sunni put on a shimmery tank top to match her Jimmy Chooz, a pair of tight jeans that complimented her hourglass figure and headed back to the party.

Sunni went to the bar to order a drink. As she sipped her drink, her eyes scanned the dance floor. Brittany must be taking a break. She was probably hugged up with some dude. Sunni checked her phone but there was to response to the text that she sent Bri. That was strange she thought, as she finished her drink. She asked the bartender if he had seen the woman that she came in with. He said that Brianna had ordered another drink and he didn't see the pretty blonde anymore. The club would be closing soon. Sunni went to the ladies' room but no sign of Brianna. Sunni got this sick feeling in the pit of her stomach as she covered every inch of the floor looking for

Bri. Sunni wondered if Bri had hooked up with some dude. But she would have text her to say that she had left the club. Sunni banged on Brianna cabin door hoping that she was knocked out from too much partying. Her knocks went unanswered. Sunni went back to her cabin and tried to get some rest. Her sleep was anything but restful. Sunni tossed and turned in anticipation of morning. Sunni rang Brianna's phone early but there was no answer. She text Bri but there was no response. Sunni showered, dressed, and went to Brianna's cabin but still got no response. Her gut told her something was wrong. She decided to go to security and tell them that Bri was missing. But what if she hooked up with some guy, it would be lame to draw attention to that. Forget that her friend was missing, she was going to do whatever necessary to find her. Sunni decided to go to the security officers and report Brianna missing.

The ship officials didn't seem to take Sunni seriously. It was suggested that Brianna was either recovering from partying the night before or maybe she had found a new friend. Sunni grew

angry as they seem to placate her instead of

taking Brianna's missing as a serious issue.

Finally, the security chief agreed to check

Brianna's cabin. As they opened the door to

the cabin, Sunni was nervous as to what they

would find. Her bed had not been slept in

the night before. Sunni checked the

bathroom, and her washcloth and toothbrush

were dry as it never used. "There is

something wrong here. Brianna has not been

here since last night. And I don't see the

clothes that she wore either!" Sunni

surmised. "We 'll begin searching the ship

immediately", the chief of security agreed.

This could take quite some time with a ship

this size. We will be in Cozumel in a few

hours said the chief. "And! I suggest you

get started," Sunni hissed, agitated that the

chief had time for excuses.

An intensive search began to locate Brianna,

meanwhile Sunni traced their steps from

last night hoping to find a clue that could

lead to her missing friend.

Sunni went to the bar in the club but there

was a different bartender. She pulled out

her phone to ask the bartender if he had

seen Brianna. He had not seen her, but

someone had turned in a cell phone. It was Brianna's smartphone, and it was cracked. Sunni was convinced more than ever that Brianna had run into foul play. Brianna was attached to her phone at the hip and wouldn't just leave it in the club. Sunni decided to see if the captain would notify the Coast Guard so the search would be escalated. Things were not moving fast enough for her. As she headed for the bridge, Sunni saw Miguel from a distance and called to him. He looked at her then quickly disappeared before she could get to him. She ran to catch up to Miguel, but he was gone. That's weird she could swear he saw her. Well, she would catch up to him after she spoke the captain. Captain Woods was more than forth coming with the progress of the search for Brianna. Sunni was anxious to find out if the Coast Guard would be searching the waters. Maybe Brianna had fallen overboard and was clinging to life in the turbulent waters. Captain Woods had assured Sunni that everything was being done to find Brianna. "Not enough is being done, Brianna is like a sister to me, and it is not like her to disappear like this. I found her phone in the bar and I am sure that something is wrong. Are you gonna help me find her or do I have to call the FBI?", Sunni warned. "Please, calm down we will find her!", the captain reassured Sunni as he put his arm around Sunni to console her. Sunni weakens when the captain

pulled her close. She allowed her vulnerability to take control momentarily as he hugged her. She rested her head on the captain shoulder briefly before

something caught her eye. His lips brushed against hers drawing her into a sweet kiss. Momentarily Sunni was distracted and had to force herself back to reality.

"I can't. I have to find my friend, Sunni

voice trailed. "What's in that room? She

asked. "What?" The captain questioned

slightly confused. "The locked door, what's

behind it?" Sunni asked. The captain

regained his composure and walked towards

the door. "Just supplies, would you like to

see?" He said and he grabbed for the keys.

A crew member came running into the

quarters claiming that there was

something in the water. They all quickly ran

to see what was being recovered. It turned

out to be a dead animal carcass.

Sunni was determined to find Bri but nothing

was panning out. She went looking for

Miguel. They had docked in Cozumel, but

she wasn't thinking about sightseeing Miguel

had acted weird and she was on her way to

see him. The spa was empty. Sunni turned

on the light and looked around. She thought

it was strange that the door was unlocked

as if someone had left in a hurry. She

searched the massage room for anything

that could be a clue. Sunni scanned the

room, spotted the linen closet, and opened

it. There was nothing there but an empty

basket for towels and such. There was a

strange odor emanating from the basket.

Upon further inspection, Sunni noticed a

long blonde hair. It looked like it could be

Brianna's hair color but that meant nothing.

They did have massages there. She placed

the hair in her pocket and left. She had a

gut feeling that Miguel knew something and

she had to find him. Sunni went to the

captain to question him about his crew

members. She wanted to get info on Miguel

and maybe the captain could help. Miguel

was not on his list of crew members. The

captain assured Sunni that he would find out

why someone would be massaging

guests who was unauthorized to be there. Sunni needed a drink and decided to check out the bars in hopes that she would run into Miguel. As she sipped her drink, deep in thought, her thoughts were interrupted by a voice she had heard before. It was Francois down the bar talking to bartender.

He seemed to be getting faded and she wondered if she could get any information from him. Sunni eased into a closer bar seat and ordered a drink. Francois noticed her and turned to her. "Hello, gorgeous! Can I buy you another one?" Francois suggested. He was clearly feeling no pain. It occurred to Sunni that maybe he was drinking to

forget something. "Maybe... when I finished

this one. You remember me?", she asked.

"Hell, yeah! You and your friend... the

hottest chicks on this ship. Hey, any word

on her yet?', Francois asked. He nodded to

the bartender to give Sunni another drink.

She sipped the drink slowly pondering the

change in Francois's not so thick French

accent. "No, to answer your question. I

think the Coast Guard have begun searching

the waters. I just pray they'll find my friend

and she's okay...you know," Sunni

rationalized. "Hey, don't you worry your

pretty little head, I'm sure your friend is fine." Francois tried to reassure Sunni as he put his arm around her to console her. She eased out of his embraced and reached for another drink. Sunni was feeling pretty good, but she had to focus. This fake ass Frenchman knew something, and she was gonna get it out of him. Sunni poured on the charm. Before long they were laughing and Francois telling her how popular he and Miguel were with the ladies. Miguel was down on his luck, so Francois got him on the ship to help with his massage gig. He had gotten off the ship in Cozumel. It was

something to do with his family.

 Francois was sweating her to come back to

his cabin since his friend was gone, they

could be alone. Sunni was making excuses

and playing hard. Sunni knew if she got

Francois alone, she could find out something

that could lead her to Brianna's

whereabouts. When the bartender waited on

other patrons and Francois had turned his

head, Sunni would pour drinks down the drain

behind the bar.

She wanted to sober up but give Francois

the appearance that she was fucked up. As

they walked to his cabin, he grabbed her ass

and Sunni let him. As he opened the door to

his cabin, Francois was pawing her. He

sucked at her neck and forced his tongue in

her mouth. Sunni struggled to maintain her

composure but snapped back when his hand

ripped at her jeans. She instinctively

elbowed Francois and came back with

a punch to the head that knocked him to his

cabin bed. He was knocked out and probably

wouldn't remember this in the morning. She

sighed that her kick boxing had paid off.

Realizing that his phone was in his pocket,

Sunni needed to retrieve it. She eased her

fingers into his snug pants. They brushed

against his penis. Damn, Francois she

thought, you are hung...horny bastard. She

grasped the phone and tipped into the

bathroom. His contact list was still up so

Sunni quickly looked for Miguel's info. He

had left the ship, but she had a gut feeling

that he knew something. She found his,

name, number and noted the word Juarez.

Quickly she entered it into her phone,

dropped the phone on the bed and tipped out

of the cabin before Francois came to. Sunni

got back to her cabin totally wired.

She jumped into the shower to relax so she could go to sleep. As the water ran over her body, she thought about all that was happening. She felt anxious and alone. She was about to sleuth around Cozumel trying to locate Miguel. She had no idea if she would find him or if he even knows anything. She just knew that shit was falling apart. Her man was gone, her best friend was missing, and she was in a foreign land trying to find her. Her emotions took over her and she began to weep uncontrollably.

The water saturated her beautiful body. The steady stream hit her nipples making them erect as her hand drifted down to

clitoris. Sunni worked her clit until her body

convulsed. She moaned in ecstasy as the

orgasmic pulsations flooded through her

entire body. She regained her composure,

dried off, lotioned up and tried to get some

sleep. She had an arduous journey to find

her friend.

Cozumel

Sunni had heard that Cozumel was beautiful

with white sandy beaches, crystal clear,

warm water, and great scuba diving. Sunni

had always wanted to try scuba diving. She

really should be more adventurous she

thought as she drifted to sleep.

Sunni had taken all of her luggage as well as

Brianna things off the ship. She had no

intentions of going back on the ship and

Brianna would need her stuff when she

found her. Maybe she was living in denial,

but she was going to do all in her power to

find her friend. She had checked with

security about updates on the search.

There was no news on Brianna. Sunni rented

a hotel room in Cozumel, Mexico at a quaint

hotel called Casa Maya. It looked like a

travel brochure with an inviting courtyard

lavish with flowers and tropical plants. The

pool seemed to call her name and it was

littered with tourists lounging, laughing, and

drinking. Sunni hoped at some point she

would get to really enjoy the ambiance. As

Sunni sat on the firm bed of her

comfortable room, she contemplated her

next move. She looked at Miguel's number in

her contacts. She pondered Brianna's phone

remembering that a picture of Miguel was in

her phone. Sunni called the phone, and it

rang. Glad that the phone wasn't broken,

she began trying to figure out the password.

She tried every possibility she could think

that Brianna would use. She tried Brianna's

name, birthdate, address, even her family

names. On a goof, Sunni input innus and the

phone opened. Sunni smiled that was

her girl. Brianna had used her named as the

password. Dammit closer than sisters. Or

maybe my name she would remember even if

she were totally faded.

Sunni found the picture of Miguel in

Brianna's phone. It was time to find out

what Miguel knows. Brianna had gotten

Miguel's last name Rodriguez from Francois.

But who or what was Juarez? She called

Miguel's number but there was no answer.

Sunni decided it was time to loosen up. She

put on a cute, yellow string bikini that totally

accented her cinnamon skin. Heads turned as

she selected a lounge chair, placed a towel

down on the chair and began to apply

sunscreen. A waiter can over to her quickly.

He was happy to take her order as he

admired her beauty. Sunni ordered a

Margarita to sip while she socialized. She

would charm her way into finding out where

the locals hang out.

 Sunni had fun socializing with tourists and

locals. Although language barriers were

not a problem, Sunni had fun speaking

Spanish as she charmed her way into

obtaining information. The taxicab company

was in close proximity, so Sunni decided to

go sightseeing. This was a small island, and

someone probably knew Miguel Rodriguez

and could tell her where to find him.

The waiter had mentioned a popular local

hangout called Charlita and Carlos in "town".

That's a popular hangout of the bars and restaurants that locals frequently went. Sunni put on an asymmetrical, coin embellished, scoop neck, red blouse with shorts and metallic, snakeskin wedges. Who cares if they were knockoffs? She rolled up to Charlita and Carlos's looking hot as hell. Sunni was glad that she took Bri's advice and cashed in Mark's ticket. Gin and tonic in hand, Sunni explored the club. The club had a restaurant, three bars, billiards, and media room. She had Bri's phone with Miguel's picture in it. She hadn't seen

him, but she could show it to the locals to

see if any one recognized Miguel.

Sunni grabbed a drink and sauntered to the

billiards table hoping to attract attention

and play a friendly game. As she racked the

balls, a sexy local guy approached her to see

if she wanted to play a game. "I'll play you

for drinks mami", he said. Sunni thought for

a second, she had to keep her wits about

her. "How about dollar a ball? She replied.

"Oh, shit! Mami got game...si. Rack 'em up,

the local said. Sunni proceeded to beat the

pants off the guy. He peeled off two

hundred bucks and with a sly smile to her.

"Damn baby, you gotta give me a chance to

win some of my money back", the local said.

"Why should I? I don't even know you.

"What's your name?" Sunni asked. "Mi

nombre es Juaez." He replied in Spanish.

Sunni looked perplexed so Juaez continued

the conversation in English. It was no harm

in him thinking that she was oblivious to the

language. "So... how about it? I'll show you

around a little. There is a place called Club

22 where there are all kinds of gambling.

You are pretty-smart chica. We'll have some

drinks, some laughs and maybe I'll win some

of my money back," he pressed.

Sunni's mind was racing as she agreed to

hang with him. Could this be the same

Juarez that was in Francois's phone? She

had to take a chance and find out. They

took a taxi to the club. Juarez pulled out

money to pay the taxi and Sunni turned her

head pretending to check out the sites.

Juarez was not as broke as he seemed.

They walked into the club and were

immediately greeted by beautiful wait staff

who were happy to take their orders. It was

a diverse combination of people, sounds and

music that flooded her senses.

Sunni became a kid in a candy shop not sure

of what she wanted to do first. She and

some college friends had tried to break the

bank in Las Vegas at the roulette, but Sunni

felt she had a knack for blackjack. With

drink in hand, she went to the blackjack

table. Juarez was on her ass, watching her

moves. Sunni managed to win 4 thousand

dollars before the dealer was changed.

Juarez smile at her. "Damn baby you are on

fire. I thought there was something special

about you," he boasted. "You ain't seen

nothing yet. It's 'bout to get hotter in this bitch!" Sunni beamed as she walked towards the roulette tables. Juarez gently grabbed her armed and kissed her lips. He whispered in her ear to take the money that he slipped into her hand. He wanted her to flip it into more money.

She took the money and went to the roulette table to place her bets. Sunni really was on fire hitting every number she bet. It was as if there was a crystal ball in her hand. Grinning from ear to ear she looked up and noticed a small crowd watching her moves. She glanced around but did not see Juarez. There was one face that

seemed familiar but when she tried to get

closer for a better look, he disappeared into

the crowd. Sunni decided to go cash in her

winning and find Juarez. She collected her

money and turned to find Juarez and there

he was standing close, invading her personal

space. She peeled off a grand and gave it to

him.

"That's all you get for taking off!", she

smiled. Oh baby, you know the way to a

man's heart. Let me make sure you get

home. This can be a dangerous place,"

Juarez teased in a seemingly

thicker Latino accent. Sunni was no closer

to finding out who he really was and decided

that she may have to get to know Juarez on

a deeper level. "You're being seriously

attentive, where is your girlfriend? I mean,

I don't see a ring. A man as fine

as you has to have someone...a man?," Sunni

teased. Juarez laughed a deep hearty laugh.

"There ain't nothing gay about me. I can

show you if you like," he replied. They both

laughed as she suggested they go to Casa

Maya and put her money in the safe. In the

morning, she would bank it but for now...she

had plans for Juarez. By the time that they

got to Sunni's hotel it was late but not too late for drinks. They went to the lounge, pounded tequila shots and jammed to the Latin music. Juarez was light on his feet, spinning Sunni around and dipping her like she was his puppet. Sunni was laughing as he pulled her body tight and tasted her sweet lips mixed with tequila. She was turned all the way up and wanted him now. They made a hasty retreat to her room and practically tore each other's clothes off. He quickly unleashed Sunni's bra as he drove his tongue deep into her mouth. She sucked hungrily at his tongue as she groped his penis. It was

hard and substantial. "Wait," she moaned
and pulled a condom out of her makeup bag
on the dresser. Juarez quickly put it on and
pulled her onto the bed. He savored the
taste of her nipples, sucking and lapping at
them eagerly as he slowly made his way to
her clitoris. Her weak whimpers began
stronger and stronger with every stroke of
his tongue.

Sweet release was imminent when he
stopped and forced his strong, hard cock in
her vagina. She wailed with pleasure as he
thrust

over and over until they both hollered with

pleasure. Exhausted they passed out in

ecstasy.

Sunni woke up 4 in the morning parched and

slightly confused. She looked over to see

Juarez still lying-in bed asleep. Quietly, she

searched his pants for a cell phone, wallet,

or anything that may have been a clue to who

he is or Brianna's whereabouts.

His cell phone was on lock and Sunni had no

clue of the password. He had no wallet in his

pocket only a piece of paper. She heard

Juarez stir in the bed and held her breathe.

Her cover would be blow if he saw her going

through his pockets. She tipped into the

bathroom to get a better look at the paper.

It was a series of numbers "21° 8' N, 86°

44' W" but what could it mean Sunni

thought. She quickly got her liner and a

piece of towel paper and copied the

numbers. She would study it later. She

quietly crept back into bed and closed her

eyes. She was contemplating her next move

and wondering if all closed eyes are sleep.

Sunni had fallen back to sleep, but she

awakens to find that she was alone. She

jumped up and ran to check the safe in her

room. All the money was still there, but

Juarez was gone. Her head pounded after a

wild night of partying. She needed coffee

and food. She took a long shower, got

dressed, grabbed her money so she could

deposit in her account. She found a good

place to eat. As she sat at the restaurant

drinking her coffee, she looked at the paper.

What could it be? It was not a phone

number...maybe

some sort of coordinates, she thought.

Sunni decides to call Captain Woods to see

if there was any news of Brianna and ask for

his help.   The captain informed Sunni that

the coast guard had covered several

hundred miles and there was no sign of

Brianna. The search had been called off.

The news was not going to stop

Sunni from her search. She refused to give

up until she had exhausted all avenues. She

asked the captain to check what she thought

may be coordinates for her. Sunni had been

right, the numbers that were in Juarez's

pocket were coordinates for Cancun.

The strange part, the captain added was

that it was in the Caribbean seas not

actually on land. The captain asked Sunni

where she had gotten the coordinates from,

but she refused to tell him. He asked if

there was anything else that he could do to

help her. Sunni said there was not. However,

she wanted to know how far the coordinates

were from Cancun inland. He told her that

the coordinates were only a few miles and

could be reached by ski boat. The captain

gave Sunni his cell phone number just in case

she needed to reach him right away. She

sensed the concern in his voice and assured

him that she would be fine. Sunni thought

to herself that it was time to figure out

what connection Juarez has to Cancun.

Sunni decided that she would need to stay at

Casa Maya for a few more days. She

remembers the hair sample that she had

kept and sent to one of her colleagues to do

a rush DNA comparison with the hair from

Brianna's hairbrush. Sunni shipped all

Brianna's luggage to her friend to hold

except for some choice outfits. It was time

for her to step up her search and she need

to be able to move at a moment's notice.

She checked with the Mexican authorities

to see if a Caucasian woman had been found

but there were no reports. She also

checked with the hospitals but no woman

fitting her description was a patient in them.

Cancun

Sunni knew that she needed to reconnect with Juarez to discover what if anything, he knew. In her mind, she dismissed the fact that he fucked her like a beast. He was smooth but shady and she knew it.

Sunni decided to return to Club 22 to see if Juarez was there. She dressed in a killer designer off shoulder, pink, embellished dress with Medusa pumps to match. They belong to Brianna, there was no way she could afford such high dollar clothing.

Maybe so when she started her big-time research position.

Sunni walked into the club like she owned the place. The waitress brought her a drink and as she sipped on it. Sunni overheard security tell one of the dealers to go replace another dealer. He said that Mr. Juarez thought the customer might be counting cards.

Charmingly, Sunni asked the dealer if Mr. Juarez was there because there was a matter that she needed to discuss. The dealer asked Sunni which Juarez, (the father Alberto or the son Carlito) did she need to talk with. Sunni told him that she

wanted to speak with Carlito. Sunni

sauntered over to the table with the

cheating customer and saw a man whose face

was familiar. She was trying to recall how

she knew him when Carlito Juarez walked up.

"Are you stalking me?" Carlito asked with a

sneaky smile.

"No... but is that what a girl has to do to get

your attention? You disappeared on me

without so much as a goodbye." Sunni

retorted. "I apologize but I am a busy man.

Let me make it up to you. We'll have dinner

and I'll take you for a ride. How does that

sound?" He asked Sunni. "Interesting but I don't know anything about you. Like for instance the fact that you own this place and never told me. What other secrets do you have?" She questioned. "You're very inquisitive, my sweet. Come with me," Carlito said as took her hand and guided her to a private dining area. They dined on lobster as he told Sunni that he had several businesses that require his attention. That had been the reason that he left so abruptly the other morning. Dinner was exquisite but Carlito topped it off with a drive on his boat. The sun was beginning to set on the tropical paradise as they glided in the turquoise ocean towards Cancun. It was really close about 50 miles and they reached inland in no time. The pier was littered with restaurants, clubs and businesses. As they walked a short way down the pier, Sunni asked if Carlito owned any of the businesses that they encountered. He was slightly evasive saying one or two. Sunni looked around trying to remember her surroundings. "My feet are starting to hurt with these heels on. Let's go into this establishment and get a cool drink," Sunni posed. Carlito agreed and they went into Bar None, a small watering hole to chill out. It looked like a scene from Casa Blanca with quaint little tables, hanging lights and tropical plants. "So, how long will you be in town? You're quite a woman and I like hanging out with you," Carlito charmed. "I'm not sure but I have had a great time. Maybe, I'll stay a little longer," Sunni said as she slyly smiled. "Good then we can stay in Cancun and go snorkeling tomorrow. You do know how to snorkel, right!" he inquired. "Actually, I've never been, and I don't have a swimming gear." Sunni said reluctantly. She had promised herself that she would live life more especially with her best friend missing.

Life is too short to sit on the sidelines. "I

got you," Carlito promised in his most

convincing Latin accent. "We will go shopping

in the morning and I know a great spot for

snorkeling. It will be really fun", he beamed.

The spot that Carlito had in mind was in

Bahia Mujures. Its white sandy beaches and

turquoise blue waters were breath taking.

Sunni was nervous and excited all at once.

They grabbed coffee and went shopping for

bathing suits, snorkeling and scuba gear.

Sunni kept her bathing suit on straight out

of the dressing room so that when they took

the boat to Bahia Mujures, she would be

ready to go. She had a cover up over top her

suit instinctively Carlito smiled knowing what

was underneath, the cover up. Sunni felt the

warmth of the sun on her face and the wind

in her hair as the boat zipped through the

waves. They arrived at the beach and the

ambiance was laid back. There were

beachgoers but the beach wasn't crowded.

Sunni drew attention when she removed her

cover to reveal her perfectly proportioned

body. The yellow bikini that she wore

accented her curves,

She looked like sunshine and Carlito could

hardly contain himself as he tried to give

Sunni scuba lessons. She was a quick learner

and was ready to literally swim with the fish.

The day was an incredible adventure. She

saw the most colorful array of fish that she

had ever seen before. Sunni had never seen

the reefs and they were unbelievable Sunni

took pictures with her camera phone. She

was glad that she spent the money for

 a good waterproof phone.   She could not

wait to download them on her laptop later.

Sunni was exhausted when they came back

to shore so, they rested under an

umbrella with a tropical drink. As she looked

at her pictures, she noticed that she had

several messages. She needed to get by

herself so that she could listen to them.

She was hoping that her friend from the

laboratory had results for her. She

disregarded the 10 messages from Mark.

But Sunni was anxious to open the message

from her laboratory colleague. Carlito went

to the boat to make some calls. Sunni

thought that was strange, but it gave her an

opportunity to read the colleague's findings.

The hair was not from Bri but it belongs to a

younger female. Sunni was anxious to get

back to her room to do some research on

her laptop.   She made an excuse to Carlito

that she was feeling ill and need to go back

to the island and rest. He was fine with

that and once back in Cozumel she took a

cab to her hotel. Once back, Sunni searched

for any records on the Juarez name and

found more than she bargained for. It

appears that the name is connected to

organized crime. They not only owned

several businesses that were believed to be

fronts for the crime lords but there had

been many arrests. However, authorities could not make any convictions for drugs and malicious wounding stick. Sunni was anxious that she had been hanging with some bad men. It is no wonder that Carlito had so much money to throw around.

Knowing what kind of men, she was dealing with, did not deter her from continuing

to search for Brianna. She researched the ship to see if there could have been any other disappearances. Oddly enough, there were missing person cases in which the FBI had been brought into the search.

It was time to step up the game!

Under Cover

When sightseeing before in Cozumel, Sunni had remembered going down back streets off the main strips. You could buy anything your heart desired. The vendors would even offer free shots of tequila as you browsed the stores. She decided to return and procure some protection. She had studied kickboxing and was well trained, but she knew that she needed some heat. She put on some comfortable jeans, a loose-fitting top and a money belt up under the top. She did want to look too touristy.

Sunni pretended as she went from shop to shop that she wanted to buy jewelry. She finally came across a pawn shop. It had just what she was looking for. She found a 45 caliber that fit nicely in her hand. The owner wanted a ridiculously low price for it, so she purchased it along with some ammunition. Sunni had plenty of money left to work with so, her gut feeling told her that she should go back to Cancun. Sunni's first thought was to rent a boat for the day but that could draw attention to her. She decided to take the ferry like the other tourists for now. She traveled with other tourists initially but ventured off into the seedy areas of the city. She talked with locals and eventually got the nerve to ask about purchasing some weed. The local guy looked to be about 18. He asked her if she was police or something. Sunni responded that she was not law enforcement and just wanted to catch a buzz while in town. He reluctantly agreed to hook her up for a small fee. He told her to meet him at a bar around the corner in 30 minutes. Sunni found the bar and took a seat at a booth where she had clear visibility of her surroundings. It took forever for the kid to come back Sunni thought. She was starting to feel butterflies in her stomach. . .

Maybe he was setting her up to rob her. She saw a couple of Latino dudes come in, but they seem to avoid looking in her direction.

Sunni got up to leave and tried to get a look at the dudes. She was n't for sure but one of the guys looked like Miguel. Sunni went around the corner but still had a view of the bar. She pulled out the cell phone to look at Miguel's picture. It was him with a cap on his head! She waited and saw them coming

out the bar as the local weed dealer went in

the bar. They seem to know each other

judging by the way they greeted each other

and held a lengthy conversation. Sunni

contemplated whether to follow them or to

see if she could get information out of the

dealer. She decided that the element of

surprise may be better. She would get the

information from the dealer. He was a wiry

but cute and Sunni somehow felt oddly

comfortable with him. She asked him where

they could go to complete the transaction.

Sunni really wanted to get him to smoke with

her and find out Miguel's hangout. "So, you
don't trust me?" the dealer asked. "I don't
know you! What's your name anyway?" Sunni
inquired. My name is Pablo, how about you?
She contemplated lying but the truth was
easier to keep up with. My name is Sunni.
So, how about it? I just wanna try it and
catch a buzz before I go back to my room.
You cool with that?" Sunni asked. "Sure,
you seem like a cool chick!" Pablo agreed.
So, he took her to the room where he stayed
not far from the bar. They got to know
each other a little better while they smoke.
Pablo actually smoked more than Sunni.

While she tried not to inhale too much. She

had to keep some of her wits. Sunni told

him that she hoped that she ran into her

friend Miguel since she would only be in town

for a short time. He told her that he and

Miguel were tight, and he could give her the

address. She played it off but that was

exactly what she wanted. She thanked him

for the hook up, paid him and left. Sunni

felt sure that Miguel knew something. She

caught a cab to the address that Pablo had

given her. She asked the driver to put her

off a couple blocks from the address. The

area seemed unsavory. Sunni stomach had

butterflies as she got closer to her

destination. Chicas yelled at her asking if

she was lost because she was in the wrong

place. Sunni patted the piece in the pack

under her blouse feeling slightly more

secure. The address that she approached

appeared to be a warehouse. Sunni tried to

look in the window, but it was darkened out.

It had gotten dark, so she used her lighter

to see. Heart pounding Sunni crept around

the back. The warehouse had a bay door

that was not completely shut. She looked

around for something to pry it open with

just enough to crawl inside. Sunni had

officially "broke and entered". If Miguel

was there, she was sure that he could hear

the loud beat of her heart. It was dimly lit

so Sunni quickly surveyed her surroundings.

Suddenly she heard footsteps. Make sure

you bring back a good bottle of tequila. None

"of the cheap shit," one man instructed

the other as he left. Sunni quickly hid

behind some boxes praying that she had not

made any noise. As the door shut behind the

man, Sunni slowing crept towards the voice

that she heard. She unzipped her pack as

she crept closer. Suddenly someone

grabbed her from behind. .

Sunni squealed in surprise "What the fuck

are you doing here? He asked. She

recognized the voice. "Please don't hurt me,

Miguel!" Sunni pleaded. He held her tight as

he turned up the lights for a closer look at

her. As he did so she caught him off guard

with an elbow to his ribs. He fell as she

quickly grabbed her gun. She pointed it at

him. "I don't want to hurt you. I'm looking

for my friend. I know you remember her.

The pretty blonde from the ship. "Where is

she?", Sunni demanded. He smiled. "I

swear I will put a bullet in your eye if you

don't tell me what happened to her", Sunni

threatened. "You'll never find her", Miguel

said as he regained his composure and stood

to his feet. He began walking closer as he

talked to her. "You've got some balls coming

here. You don't know who you are fucking

with. Now give me the gun!", Miguel said

gruffly. "I'm warning you", Sunni yelled. Her

warning went unheard as he lunged for the

gun. Sunny pulled the trigger and caught

Miguel in the shoulder. The bullet went

straight through but he hollered in pain and

fell to the floor. She yelled to him that she

was sorry and ran to help him. Dammit, I did

not want to shoot you! Now, where is

Brianna?" as she stuck her finger in the hole

in his shoulder. "She's gone!", he hollered.

"Gone where!" Sunni pursued questioning.

"They moved her to another location for the

buyer!" Miguel shouted through the pain.

"What the hell are you saying?", Sunni

pursued questioning. "I'm saying you are

mixed up in some very bad shit," Miguel

yelled. The door opened and Andres, his

partner walked in holding a bottle of tequila.

"What the hell is going on?", Andres shouted

as he reached for his piece. "Drop it and

kick it over to me!" Sunni shouted forcefully,

pointing her gun at him. "Do as she says and

bring me that bottle. This shit hurts!".

Miguel barked orders as he cursed

obscenities in Spanish. Miguel snatched

the bottle and took big gulps to ease the

pain. Sunni holding both guns insisted on the

truth. "I can stop the bleeding and stitch

that up but I'm not doing shit until you tell

me where Brianna was taken. Well?" She

stood over the men with guns cocked. "Hey

this isn't something that I am proud of, but

I owe no, we owe a debt to Mr. Juarez. In

exchange for letting us live, we pay him back

with interest.

"My dumbass brother lost 10 kilos of heroin. So, we gotta pay it back. We do whatever shit job Juarez wants done. Right, now he's shipping girls to the highest bidder. They get missing off the ship and nobody is the wiser. They think the girls go overboard. Your sexy friend is worth millions. We figure this last job should pay our debt to Juarez", Miguel said taking another gulp. He was fucked up and suddenly forthcoming. "Motherfuckers ! How can you do this to innocent women?", she yelled. "You run your fucking mouth too much. Mr. Juarez is gonna kill us," Andres shouted. Impulsively, he took a run at Sunni, and she dropped him

to the floor with a kick to the head. Andres

fell like a potato sack, Miguel was drunk and

no threat so Sunni quickly scrounged around

for something to sew up Miguel,

She didn't want him bleeding out. She found

all kinds of drugs in the warehouse. Sunni

wondered what she had gotten herself into.

She couldn't stop now. At least, she knew

that Brianna was still alive. But how did they

get Brianna off the ship without anyone

knowing. She wondered if Francois was

involved and who else was a party to such

heinous crimes. She asked Miguel how they

got Brianna off the ship. Miguel revealed

that he waited until the target would be

so fucked up that she can be easily

manipulated. If the target wasn't a heavy

drinker, then, she would be drugged. They

chose single women traveling alone but could

only kidnap one per cruise to avoid drawing

attention. Miguel kept drinking and talking as

Sunni sewed up his shoulder. He disclosed

that BJ would help get the target from the

ship on to a waiting speed boat.

They were brought to the warehouse for a

short time while transport to the buyer was

arranged. "Who is BJ?", Sunni asked as she

finished closing the wound. One of Mr.

Juarez' s"men is all I know. I ain't

never seen his face. He could be anybody

for all I know." Miguel slurred. His head

wobbled from total intoxication. "Where

can I find him? Maybe he knows where they

took Brianna," Sunni thought. "Juarez own

some businesses like clubs, casinos and

restaurants. Check one of them, Miguel said

as he took another swig of tequila. Sunni

took her gun from out her belt and quickly

moved towards the door. Andres still lay

knocked out on the floor and Miguel at this

point was too fucked up to care. Sunni

considered the places that Miguel suggested

and figured that the casinos might be a good

place to start.

The Hunt

Sunni was exhausted when she got back to

Cozumel. She was able to catch a late ferry

and passed out from fatigue. She was too

tired to contemplate the tumultuous night

and quickly fell into REM sleep. When Sunni

awoke, it was 3 in the evening, and she was

starving. Her instincts told her that it might

be smart to change hotels. She did so,

used a different name and paid for extra

days in advance.   She dressed in evening

attire after deciding to hit the casinos. She

put on one of Brianna's stunning designer

dresses. The dress she chose was a teal, knee length, sweetheart sequin adorned at the breast, Versace. The free flowing material made it easy to strap the piece to her thigh and it go undetected. The gradient heel, peep toe, Jimmy Chooz set off the outfit. Sunni went to a couple of casinos, but they were dead, so, she eventually returned to Club 22. Sunni grabbed a bite to eat, some poker chips and headed for the roulette table. She wondered if her luck would hold out in more ways than one. Her bank account was still looking sweet but there is always room for improvement. Her real concern was the whereabouts of Brianna. She watched the table for a while sipping on her favorite vodka tonic. Lady luck was on her side when she bet on black 13 and won. She collected her winnings and was about to place another bet when out of the corner of her eye she spotted someone staring at her. She looked around intensely for this male figure, thinking that it may have been Carlito. Sunni cashed in her winnings in a check. She secured her money in the casino safe. Sunni would get it later. Right now, the search was on to find the mystery man.

She hastened through the guests in the casino, trying to avoid attention.

Sunni saw no one of interest so she decided to go to the ladies' room to freshen up. She made sure everything was tight including that piece that she had safely stashed away. She opened the door to proceed out of the ladies' room when she saw a familiar face. She was about to get his attention when her phone rang. She didn't look at the caller ID just answered in a slightly irritated voice. "Hello?" Sunni answered. "Can you hear me, I've been trying to call you! Are you alright?"

questioned the voice on the other end. "I, I

can't talk right now. Gotta go!" Sunni said

abruptly,

She turned the phone off, quickly tucking it

safely in her bra. Calls at the wrong time

could get her ass knocked off, she thought

as she spied the man.

She saw the man dip into one of the rooms

and followed. Her hand grasped the knob

and as she turned it, security approached

Sunni asking if she was lost. She smiled

coyly..."I guess I am. I have to powder my

nose," she replied as she danced from side

to side. "Miss let me show you where to go.

This area is for employees," the guard said

as he guided her out of the area. Sunni

made a mental note. As soon as she was out

of security's eyesight, she would find out

who was behind the doors.

Suddenly alarms went off as a lucky player

hit the jackpot. Sunni ducked behind a door

and quickly slid through while security

rushed to the excitement. One guard came

back to punch a code and alert the boss that

he was needed. She had hidden behind a

large plant but had a vantage point to see

the code. The door quickly opened, and

Sunni ducked as she heard footsteps leaving the room. She eased up and quickly ran to the door and punched in the codes. Maybe there was something in the office that would lead her to Brianna.

As Sunni opened the door, she heard a hardy laugh of a familiar voice. "Well, well, well my beautiful amore. I wondered when you would find your way back to me, Carlito said dubiously. He reeked of bravado as he eased toward her, pulled her close and tasted her lips. He slid his tongue between her lips and Sunni's knees buckled slightly. "I was really starting to feel for you, but you do not respect me as a man. You run around my city, snooping in things you know nothing about. Did you think I would not find out? I know everything that goes on," he barked clearly agitated. "Carlito, you don't understand, I'm trying to find my friend. She has been missing for days and I have to find her", Sunni pleaded. "I was planning to bust a cap in that beautiful dome. You have infiltrated my business too deeply. But, I have tasted you sweet nectar and I have a much more profitable use for you," Carlito promised. The door opened, suddenly. "Ah, let me introduce you to my compadre" ...BJ.

This is Sunni", Carlito said. Sunni turned and

recognized that face staring back. BJ has

connections through his travels. This helps

me provide some very influential people with

some of the most beautiful women in the

world. This is one of my many business

markets. You should feel lucky you are about

to embark on a journey and your life spared

"Carlito explained. "Crewman Johnson?",

Sunni asked. He nodded. "Shouldn't you be

on the ship? And is Captain Woods involved

in this shit too?" She questioned. "You ask a

lot of questions. If you must know, Captain

gave me time off for a few of days.

His ass is clueless. I am the one who should

be running the ship not him. But my time is

coming. In the meantime, I am working off a

debt. If you would have minded your own

business... That's why you are in this mess,"

Johnson lectured. "You insensitive piece of

shit! You took my friend, and you think I'm

going to let this go? You don't know me,

bitch!" Sunni bellowed as Johnson moved in

to grab her. "Take her to the container!",

Carlito demanded. Johnson grabbed Sunni

and she punched the shit out of him. He

retrieved a gun from the back of his pants

and pointed. Sunni reacted, kicking it out of

his hand and to the floor. "We don't have time for this shit", Carlito said as he came from behind his desk with his arm behind his back. Sunni ran toward the door and as she grabbed the knob, she felt a sharp pain in her neck. Carlito had injected Sunni with Propofol. Sunni was out in a few seconds. He caught her before her body hit the floor. Carlito handed her off to BJ. He instructed BJ to be careful taking Sunni to the shipping container. It was already loaded on Carlito's cargo ship. Johnson had many connections and Carlito had no problem bribing custom officials to get his products into ports. The next stop is Dubai and BJ had a ship disguise

as a car carrier. But it was loaded with

women and drugs. He had an ACL carrier

funded by Carlito. BJ found a route that he

could sail to Dubai in days and not weeks. He

had dropped off women and drugs to

Carlito's clients all around the world. The

women were in compartments that were

equipped with food and water. Sunni opened

her eyes and felt her head pounding and her

throat parched. She tried to move but was

loosely chained to a huge circular sphere. It

reminded her of an animal feeder.

The Voyage

Sunni tried to focus in the dimly lit area to

see several other women similarly detained.

A fear rushed over her as she groped for

her gun. Of course, it was gone. Sunni

felt her breasts and found her cell phone

still tucked firmly away. She checked to

see if there were any bars left. It had a

half a bar left. She tried to call but there

was not enough of a signal. She looked

around at the different ethnicities,

wondering if anyone spoke English. "Anyone

know where we are? Anyone speak English?"

Sunni asked. A response from a young,

woman who said she came from a poor family and was promised a job in the US. She looked around to see the fragile, scared, beautiful, young women who were victimized by Carlito and his men. An Asian woman said she had been there for days, chained like a dog. She said she would stand up to exercise to keep her legs working. While her English was broken and accent thick, Sunni felt her fear and anger. Another woman wept as she said that she was taken while traveling on vacation. That story sounded familiar. She asked if anyone had seen Brianna as she described her. A

Ukrainian woman said she sounded familiar, but the kidnappers make sure to keep them disoriented. She met a man on the internet, and he was looking for a wife. "I wanted to go to America," the woman revealed. It was a trick she said as she recounted their meeting. They met to get acquainted, ate food and drank. Next thing she remember she is locked away." The woman recalled.

"We have got to get out of here. If we can get our hands loose then we can jump them. Who can fight with me?" Sunni asked.

There were moans and mumbling from the women. "I will!" yelled a woman with a Hispanic accent. They are

going to whore us out. I heard the captain

say. " Nosotros las haremos putas," Maria

said in Spanish but Sunni understood

what she said. Sunni racked her brain for an

idea to escape. She scratched her head and

began to run her fingers through her

tresses. When as if by magic, a bobby pin

strategically placed to hold her hair became

wonderfully apparent. She quickly began to

work the lock to break free. Frantically she

moved the bobby pin, praying that the lock

would come open. Suddenly, Sunni heard a

click, and the lock was opened. She drank

water to get herself together. Then, she

screamed in Spanish for the woman. Sunni

told her the plan to set her and the others

free. They could look for something to use

as weapons before the men came back. She

freed each woman one by one as Maria

(Hispanic woman) looked for protection. She

didn't know how long before they reached

the destination, but they had to work fast.

Some were in no condition to fight but they

found sticks, pipes anything that they could

protect themselves with. They worked

quickly when sudden footsteps descended

from the upper level. Sunni had a piece of a

wood that she pried from a pallet. She ran

behind the stairs and nodded for Maria to

do the same. One of the men yelled at the

women as he approached. "Alright bitches,

we gonna be making a drop, so we gonna be

on land in a few. I don't want no shit or you

gonna be dead bitches" but before he could

finish, Sunni bust him in the back of the

head, and he went down hard. The women

that were physically able, scrambled to hide.

Sunni and Maria ran for the deck. One

other crewman heard the noise and grabbed

his gun. By, then, the women were on deck.

The crewman fired at Maria, and it ricochet

off the pipe that she held and knocked her

back.

The push back landed Maria close to rail of

the ocean freight shipper. Maria dove into

the water with pipe in hand. Sunni quickly

reacted and did the same.

Shots rang out from the ship, but they dove

deep enough to avoid them. The women swam

for their lives. The freight shipper kept

going and the women held their breaths for

what seemed like hours. Sunni popped out of

the water. She sucked air as if it were her

last. Sunni looked around attempting to get

her composure as much as she could. Hell,

she was in the middle of an ocean, fighting

to stay alive. Her eyes darted around

searching. Where was Maria? Suddenly,

she heard water splashing violently as Maria

gasped for breath. Sunni quickly swam to

her asking if she was okay. Sunni grabbed

Maria like old friends. "Oh, dios mios the

pain!" Maria cried. Sunni could see the blood

pooling on the water's surface from a

gunshot wound in Maria's leg. "We gotta get

you to a hospital", Sunni said. In the

meantime, Sunni tore a piece of her garment

to use as a tourniquet. She hoped that it

would slow down the bleeding. She prayed

that they would be helped before Maria lost

too much blood and went into shock. She

tried to stroke with Maria's arm grasped

around her neck. Sunni could not get very

far before she had to stop in exhaustion.

She could see that Maria was getting pale

and weaker. Sunni frantically became

stroking as hard as she could. When

suddenly she could hear off the distance

what sounded like a motorboat. The women

screamed and waved to get the attention of

whomever was steering the boat. It worked

and Sunni sighed in relief as the man helped

them on the boat. He sped quickly to shore

and got them to a close by medical facility.

The owner of the boat was an older man, and

he didn't seem to speak English. Sunni

deduced that they were in some middle

eastern country from his dialect. The man

was compassionate to the woman's injury.

Although he didn't understand how they had

come to be in dire straits, he quickly got

them to Jeddah National Hospital.

Panic stricken that Maria was not

responding, Sunni screamed for a doctor.

The medical staff quickly descended on

Maria, got her into the hospital room and

quickly worked to save her. Sunni was

surprised to find out that many spoke

English. One of the nurses asked what

happen. Sunni frantically tried to fill in the

nurse. She explained that they were

kidnapped and shot at. Sunni told the nurse

that she needed to get to the American

Consulate right away, she needed answers

about Maria, and she needed to use a

charger; Sunni rambled on as if on the

fringes of delirium. The nurse took her

phone and placed it on charge. As if

omnipotent, she came back with coffee and a

sandwich. Sunni hungrily devoured the

sandwich and sucked the coffee as she paced the floor. She tried to absorb all that happen, it was a lot to deal with. Sunni prayed that Maria would pull through. Maria had her back when they had to escape. She even managed to tell the name of the tanker that they were being held captive. Sunni felt sick as DeJa'Vu took over.

Sunni felt a knot in her throat remembering the last moment with her dad. "Sunni, uh mam...I uh sorry." The doctor struggled to find the words. Sunni realizing that the doctor was talking to her gave her total attention to him. She saw the helpful nurse standing by his side and knew that it was not good. "We tried to save Maria, but she had lost too much blood. I'm sorry for your loss," the doctor regretfully said. Sunni felt sick as she melted into the chair suddenly overcome with grief, fear, and frustration that rocked her to the core. She began to sob and could not stop. "Hey, hey...I got you", said a familiar voice. He lifted her up into his arms and held her tight. Sunni recognized the deep, soothing voice and strong secure arms. "Mark?", she cried as she melted in his arms, too hurt to care how he had hurt her. Sunni struggled to gain her composure. "Baby, I'm here. Anything you

need. I'm here for you," Mark reassured

her. Mark held her tight. "What are you

doing here, Mark?" Sunni asked as she step

back. "I have been looking for you. I

wanted to apologize but when I could not

find you, I tracked your phone. I thought

that I had lost you for a while. The signal

was so weak…. But now its strong," Mark

said. His eyes were full of sincerity.

"Everything has fallen apart, Bri is missing,

we were kidnapped, shot at, and now Maria is

dead. You are standing here like all is

forgiven. What…am I just supposed to be

good with you? I don't need you or your

fucking drama! I'm gonna find Bri and bring

her home. She is the only friend that I have

been able to depend on MARK!" Sunni

screamed. As Sunni turned to walk away,

Mark grabbed her arm. "Listen to me! Yeah,

I fucked up and I am a jerk, but you need

me! So, stop being such an independent

bitch. I came halfway around the world

because I love you and I need you. I know

you still love me Sunni, don't you?" Mark

questioned. "I don't have time for this, I

have to get to the consulate, now!", Sunni

raved. "Baby, baby, I'm sorry about your

friend. I know that you did all you could,

okay? Let me help you, we will get to the

consulate and get help," Mark reasoned.

She was frustrated, tired and angry that

she had not been able to do more for Maria.

She asked the hospital to give her a few

days and she would take Maria's remains.

They left for the American Consulate

determined to find Brianna and get

retribution for Maria death.

Jeddah

Mark rented a car, so they began the trip to the consulate. They did not have far to get to the US Consulate in Saudi City Jeddah. Sunni rambled about Maria and what a soldier she had been. Maria had even managed to identify the name of the tanker that they were held on. She promised that she would make everyone responsible pay. Mark glanced at her as they drove. He wanted to tackle the elephant in the room. "Baby...baby", Mark attempted to get a word in. "I'm so sorry for all that I put you through," he apologized. Before he could say more, Sunni took over the conversation. "You should be sorry. This is all your fault. I was going to surprise you with a ticket for the cruise from hell. But you were too busy smashing someone else. Thanks to you my best friend is a sex slave God knows where. I hate you for being so fucking, egotistical, narcissistic, selfish, horny...uh. What else?" Sunni questioned rhetorically. "I get it. I'm a huge ass. If I could take it back, I would. I never want to hurt you like that again," Mark admitted regretfully. He touched her hand, and she felt the warm of his before pulling it away. Mark could feel that no matter how angry Sunni was now; they were

not over. Sunni was starting to feel some

type of way and she was glad when they

pulled up to the Consulate. Sunni went into

detail to the consulate officer. Mark

listened astounded at what the women had

been through. Sunni told the officer about

the tanker and the identifying name and

serial. She hoped that would be enough for

the authorities to apprehend the men and

rescue the women still aboard. Mark was

determined more than ever to help find

Brianna and get them back home safely.

The Consulate officer took them to the ambassador. After he heard Sunni's story, Ambassador Charles began making calls. He called the FBI and they coordinated with the captain to get all the information that they could on BJ or aka Crewmen Johnson as he was known to Captain Woods.

Sunni told the ambassador that the men were making a stop nearby. Sunni questioned if there could be a brothel or anyplace where women could be kept as sex slaves. Ambassador Charles informed them that while Jeddah was progressive in many ways, that kind of illicit behavior was frowned upon. In many areas, local women still wore bukas. There were stiff penalties for prostitution, alcohol, and drug use. The ambassador could recall a few times when Americans had come here to work. They did not educate themselves on the customs or rules. As, a result, he has saved a few from hard labor or worse for their crimes.

"Ambassador, we need to find our friend! Where do you suggest we go to let's say find "illicit behavior"?," Sunni dared asked.

"Keep in mind, Brianna is being sold for a high dollar amount according to my sources. So, who has that kind of money? And how do we get inside?", Sunni questioned. The

ambassador was quiet as he pondered Sunni's

questions. "There are quite a few rich

citizens in this country. But very few that

would dare risk their reputations and

families by involving themselves in such

dealing", the ambassador advised. "However,

I have heard of a couple of land developers

that deal with American contractors.

Perhaps, they provide other resources to

make the contractors feel "welcome", the

ambassador theorized. He wrote a couple of

names on a piece of paper

He told them that he had no jurisdiction beyond the consulate walls, but he would do whatever he could to help.

The ambassador kept his word by notifying the FBI and governing authorities in Jeddah. Sunni had provided descriptions of the traffickers as well as the vessel identification number. He would make sure that BJ would not have another opportunity to be first mate on another ship. The authorities would place BJ on the international wanted list. He would not get far.

Before Sunni and Mark left the consulate, they took advantage of the ambassador's help. Search engines were invaluable to obtain information on the names that the ambassador provided. They were also able to rent a hotel room in Jeddah that was in close proximity to the consulate.

Ambassador Charles educated them on customs and culture of Islam. He suggested that Sunni get an abaya (long black, loose-fitting dress) and a hijab to cover head and face. In some places, foreigners could get away without wearing traditional dress. Sunni was not happy with the attire. "This is medieval for women to be treated this

way...like someone's property" Sunni

complained. The ambassador interjected.

"You must understand that being Muslim is

taken very seriously here. It is their

religion...their way of life. Foreigners should

respect their ways. Ignorance can result in

bad trouble". The ambassador was stern as

he warned them. "I am so ready to find Bri

and get back home", Sunni announced. "I, you

mean we...we are doing this together. Don't

go wilding out like you can do it

all by yourself!" Mark was adamant that

Sunni understands they had to be on the

same page.

"I don't think you want to start telling me

what to do. I got this, Sunni said as she

glared at Mark. "Ambassador, you have been

extremely helpful." Sunni smiled, shook his

hand, and headed to the door. Mark stood

there for a second thinking that Sunni

dismissed what he had just said. He shook

the Ambassador hand and quickly followed

Sunni. "You really need to check your

attitude", Mark bellowed after Sunni. We

are in this together. So, chill out!" Mark

demanded. "So, let me get this straight.

I'm supposed to forget all that's happen, fall

into your arms and we are good again? No, it

doesn't work that way. My attitude will

change when it changes. When I get over

what you did then maybe we can find a way

to be friends again. But don't push me

because you suddenly want to be my

superman." Sunni was so... so serious as she

got into the car, and they headed to the

hotel. The silence was deafening so Mark

tried to lighten things up by suggesting they

get some food. He parked the car near an

open market, and they walked toward nearby

136

merchants. Sunni grabbed a scarf to cover her head.

Mark ordered some food and asked the merchant where they could purchase suitable attire for them. They purchased Falafel (a deep-fried doughnut made of chickpeas and fava beans) and lamb kabobs. The food looked appetizing, and they were famished. They ran across a vendor selling hijabs (among other things) on the way to the car. They sat in the car and ate without speaking. Mark announced that they should head to the Marriot Jeddah.

He knew that Sunni was tired, and he had jet lag himself. They went to their room. "So, how is it that we are in the same room?" Sunni inquired. "I tried to get separate rooms, but this was the only thing available. Beside...we need to have each other's backs. I think it's a good idea that we are in the same room.

At least, we have separate beds", Mark rationalized. "I have an idea. I could set up a meeting with the locals. I will record the conversations and we will listen to them. Maybe we can determine who could be trafficking women, "Mark brainstormed.

Sunni agreed. Knowing that she would not be able to get close to the men. She knew that she needed Mark. Sunni realized that Mark was right. If they were going to find Brianna, they had to work together harmoniously. She stretched out on the bed and drifted into rem sleep. Sunni awakens to find Mark gone.

She felt a sudden sting of anxiety and began to dial the phone when the door opened. "Marrkkk! Where were you?" Sunni asked. She tried not to show that she was a little freaked. Mark smiled, "Missed me uh?", he teased. Mark pulled out a pen, but it was

more than a pen. He had it bluetoothed to

his phone and pulled up the conversation

with an image of Akbar Armed. "How did

you get this? This is too cool, "Sunni

surmised. "You won't believe the sweet haul

that I have been offered to play ball. A

recruiter saw me admiring this pen and gave

it to me. Its balling, right! So.. bae, I was

hanging around the address that the

ambassador gave us, and this dude Akbar

thought that I was lost. I told him I was

here to do contract work with

computer installation. I was about finished with my business but staying to do a little site seeing. I implied that I was looking for some fun." Mark, chucked. He spoke broken English, but he understood. Especially with the help of my trusty translation app. We communicated fine." "I'll bet you did," Sunni said sarcastically. "So, what's the plan?" Sunni asked. "Well, Akbah told me about a hookah bar where the men go to "socialize" as Mark described it, he used air quotes.

"I believe that there is more than just smoking going on. Alcohol is illegal so; I think they have a secret way to get turnt up.

If they are partying, then there are women

somewhere close to party with. I'll leave you

my pen so that you can see who I am

interacting with. It has very good range.

Maybe you will see someone that you

recognize. At the very least, if things go

wrong, with the rental car ready to go, we

can dip, quick, fast and in a hurry. Sound

like a plan?", Mark questioned. "Yeahhh"...

Sunni said reluctantly. "Well, it's better

than nothing. Ok let's do this," Sunni

agreed. It was dark when they started out

on their mission. Sunni was dressed in a

black abaya and hijab with everything
covered except her eyes.

Mark dressed in traditional garb although he
knew it was not required of him. He thought
that he would fit in more with the locals.

Sunni had a sickening feeling in her stomach
as they pulled up to the hookah.

It appeared to be an average looking
storefront. Mark turned to Sunni Kiss.

for luck,"... he smiled. "Really, save it
player". Sunni said "sarcastically as she
watched Mark walk away. She was feeling
some kinda way.

She still felt Mark. But this was no time for
that shit. They had to find Bri before it
was too late. Sunni snapped back to reality
when she could suddenly hear the men in
hookah laughing and talking. Mark was in.
She could see him and quietly blew a sigh of
relief. The men ate and it appeared that
they were drinking something stronger that
tea. Sunni could not understand what they
were saying but from what she could see,
they seem to be having fun. Sunni felt
exposed as she sat waiting for a sign from
Mark.

She was crouched down enough that no one would see her. Occasionally, Sunni would pop her head up to peep if there was anybody going in the hookah that she would recognize. Nothing was going on and after a couple of hours Mark came out with a couple of men. They said something to him as they got into their vehicle and left. After the vehicle sped away, Sunni jetted to Mark as he stood swaying slightly.

"Are you okay? Cause you looked like you fucked up." Sunni surmised. "Well, I guess you just answered your own damn question then" Mark retorted with a silly grin on his face. "Dudes got turnt up man. And they

had the nerve to ask me if I wanted a

ride...I was like, hells no cause I'm taking a

cab. Hey cabbie, let's go back to the

hotel." Mark said slurring his speech. "Well,

shouldn't we follow them. Or do

something?", Sunni questioned. "No need. I

got an invitation to a special party tomorrow.

I think tonight was about checking me out to

make sure that I was cool. If we are

lucky...tomorrow they lead us to Brianna ",

Mark speculated. "We should go right now

since you have an address. It would be the

element of surprise. We could get in there,

get Briana and jet", Sunni suggested. "It's too dangerous and we need to have a plan, ok?" Mark said. He asked but in actuality, he was trying to get Sunni to listen to reason. "Fine!" Sunni was hesitant but realized that Mark made sense. She quickly got out of the hijab once they were back in the room. Mark stripped and fell onto his bed. Sunni averted her eyes from his muscular body. It was hard to pretend that she didn't want to smash him. Mark kept trying to get Sunni's attention. "So, did you see anyone that you recognized in the hookah?" Mark asked her seductively. She turned to him and suggested that he cover

up. He smiled and slid under the covers. He

could feel that Sunni still wanted him. But it

was too soon and he wasn't going to be an

asshole. He was snoring almost as quickly as

his head hit the pillow. Sunni lay awake

anxious about finding Brianna and dejected

by Mark's nonchalance. She closed her eyes

and attempted to sleep. Sunni moaned as

she felt Mark's hot breath on her neck. His

tongue slowly tracing the familiar contours

of her body. Sunni couldn't contain her

passion, rubbing herself as she demanded

Mark …. "Hey, Sunni, Sunni that's some

dream you are having! Marked guessed as he gently tapped her arm to wake her.

She awakened from her dream feeling a little sheepish. Mark snickered, "Damn, woman. You got a lot going on. Even in your dreams." He headed into the bathroom to shower. Sunni sat up and tried to compose herself. She felt silly dreaming about Mark. The dream had been so realistic. He could have at least waited until she had an orgasm before he woke her up. Sunni thought as she got up and ordered food from room service. Mark had already began to eat when Sunni immerged from the bathroom dressed and famished. "Sit down and eat

"Horny.. I mean Sunni", Mark laughed

heartily. "Bet that you were dying for me to

come out the bathroom to say that shit.

Fuck you. Mark!" "You did that already in

your hot, sex dream," Mark came back. They

both began to laugh. Sunni couldn't lie cause

the dream was too real.

Sunni was more relaxed as she sat down to

dine with Mark. They ate pita bread,

hummus, falafel and washed it down with hot

tea. "I think that we should go case the

address to check security and the layout. I

am expected to arrive around dusk so we

have time to get prepared. Are you ready

for this Sunni? This could be very,

dangerous, and I am worried for your

safety", Mark said gently. "I'm good but

thanks for your concern. Anyway, as a

precaution, I will contact the Ambassador

Charles to let him know that we have a lead

and may need his assistance. So, lets

strategize, "Sunni suggested. Sunni and

Mark agreed that this was the best way to

get Brianna back. They cased the flat in

the daylight to see Akbar's operation.

Careful to maintain anonymity, they dressed

in local attire and switched cars.

The flat was located about 45 km from

Jeddah city limits and the hotel. It looked

similar to other flats in the villages only this

one had a tall privacy wall. Mark had to lift

Sunni on his shoulders. Sunni could see with

her binoculars that the few windows visible

had bars on them. She gave Mark the

binoculars. "Any idea how we can get her out

if she's in there?" Sunni asked. Mark

thought for a few then replied, "Yep, Trojan

horse and the horse will be packing", Mark

stated. "What?", Sunni questioned. "Come

on, we don't have much time!", Mark rushed

Sunni as timing was important to the mission.

They quickly returned to the hotel.

Dressed and ready to go, Mark reached

under dresser where he had concealed a

couple of pistons. He had taped them to the

underside of the dresser to keep them out

of sight. "Where did you get those guns

around here?" Sunni asked. "Turns out that

if you've got deep enough pockets, you can

get almost anything around here. All in who

you know. So, do you know how to handle a

piece? I would not want you to shoot your

pretty, little foot off," Mark joked. "Well, I

guess that's something that you don't know

about me. Years ago, my dad taught me how

to shoot. Did you forget that he was a

cop?", Sunni knew the question was

rhetorical. "No, baby, there is nothing that

I could forget about you," Marked said.

The Mission

Sunni paid close attention to their surroundings. She considered the idea that there may be a hasty retreat from the brothel. As Mark drove the rental car, Sunni noticed housing compounds that she assumed some locals resided. There was the market and train station nearby. It grew dark as they slowly approached the flat. They agreed that Sunni would get into the trunk as they got close to the flat.

Mark had scoped out the cameras and deliberately parked, so the car was obstructed from sight. Sunni did not want to

be spotted. Mark devised a plan to lure the

guard at the door to the rental car on the

pretense that the tire was going flat. They

would have to move fast if they hoped to

find Brianna and get out unimpeded. With

the trunk of the car slightly open, Sunni

listened for Mark to make his move. The

host, Akbar greeted Mark and invited him in.

Mark's cleverly disguised video pen had come

in handy again. He scanned the room as he

looked for Brianna. Akbar offered Mark a

drink from the bar as he explained the

amenities. Mark grabbed a drink and

pretended to sip on it as the host summoned

one of the women to go get the rest of the

ladies. Mark told Akbar his situation with

flat tire and Akbar instructed the guard to

go take a look. Mark excused himself to go

show the guard the tire. Mark walked

around the car and as the guard followed, he

bust him in the back of his head. Sunni

popped from the trunk, and they moved

quickly. Mark threw the guard in the trunk,

and they quickly advanced to the house.

Mark went in and motioned for Sunni to

followed. She quickly moved towards the

upstairs as Mark distracted Akbar by

laughing and talking. Women came from

upstairs and Sunni pulled the hijab

over her face to cover her identity. She

scanned the women as they came down for

inspection. None of them were Brianna,

They were all different nationalities. When

Sunni lifted the vail of the last woman. She

gasped at her old friend. Her eyes were

cold as if she did not recognize her. She

motioned to Mark. Sunni moved Brianna

towards the door and when she was just

close enough to grab the doorknob, Akbar

yelled. "Where do you think you are

going?", he bellowed.

But before he finished the sentence, Mark

knocked him out with the butt of his gun.

He dashed to the door throwing Brianna over

his shoulder. He grabbed Sunni's hand,

practically dragging her towards the car.

The ruckus drew attention and a couple

Akbar's men came to check it out.   Mark

hustled Brianna into the backseat. Sunni

jumped in the driver 'seat and popped the

trunk. Mark threw the guard from the trunk

to the ground. The guard lay unconscious as

another of Akbar's men came running out

and attempted to grab the door open. Mark

holla. "Drive! as he kicked dude in the head

knocking him out too.

They sped down the road to the sound of

muffled gunshots. Sunni floored the gas.

She was so scared and excited at the same

time. "Are they behind us! Sunni screamed.

"No, not yet drive!" Mark yelled as he kept

his eyes peeled on the back window and

Bri. She lay on the back seat. She seemed

out of it. They devised a plan as they

got closer to the hotel. Mark would quickly

get their things, check out and they

would be on their way out of the country.

Sunni thought ahead and suggested that

they pack all their bags. Mark was to check

out while she drove to the parking deck to

switch back to the original car that

they rented. Sunni tried to reach Brianna as

they switched cars. It was a struggle to get

Bri to the other rental and into the car.

"Sweetie, Come on baby. Snap out of it. It is

me, Sunni. It's gonna be alright. Bri, we are

going get you out of here and get you help.

You'll be back to your old self in no time".

Sunni said as she lay Brianna on the back

seat.

Sunni sat in the driver's seat and drove

towards the rental office. Sunni shuttered

as she observed two men drive up to the

rental that the women had just abandoned.

"Shit, shit, shit!" Sunni cursed as she drove

the car hoping she was not noticed. Once

out of view, Sunni sped towards the main

office praying that Mark had completed

checkout and was waiting for her. She

pulled up honking the horn. She saw Mark

through the door glass as he looked up.

"Come on", Sunni shouted and waved to

Mark. Mark picked up the pace, with bags in

tow, he ran to the car. The trunk was

unlocked, and Mark threw the bags in the car. "Hurry, they are after us", Sunni yelled. A Range Rover was speeding towards them, gunshots rang out as Mark dove into the front seat. "Go, go, go", Mark hollered as Sunni floored the gas pedal. Her heart raced as they headed to the only place where they would be helped.

"Mark, call Ambassador Charles and tell him that we need help. Now!", she yelled

Sunni glanced at Mark as she drove at a dangerously high speed. "Did you hear me? Are you ok?" Sunni yelled. "I've been better, don't freak out baby but I've been shot",

Mark announced way too calmly. "What! Oh

my God!" Sunni freaked. "Baby, baby, I'm ok

just drive", Mark demanded as he frantically

looked for something to tie up his leg. A

bullet had hit Mark in his thigh.

 Mark knew he needed to stop the bleeding.

He grabbed a scarf from the back seat.

Mark quickly and efficiently tied off the

wound. He looked back to check on Brianna

as the car blazed towards the consulate.

Bullets continued to fly past the car. They

were seven kilometers from the consulate.

Mark pulled his gun from his back and

returned fire even though he was in pain. He

tried to shoot out the tires, but they were going at such a high speed that it was difficult for him to get off a good shot. Sunni felt for her phone. She bluetoothed a call into the consulate. "Hello, I need to speak to Ambassador Charles. It's an emergency, please.!," Sunni shouted. The officer put the ambassador on the phone. Sunni frantically explained. "Ambassador, this is Sunni, and we are being chased. My boyfriend has been shot, and my friend needs of medical attention, now! Ambassador, we are headed that way. "Sunni pleaded. "Sunni, I will post my men

immediately and notify International police.

A chopper will be waiting to take you and

your friends to the hospital immediately.

How far are you, Sunni?", Ambassador

asked. "I don't know about 2 km out but I

gotta go," Sunni shouted as the clang of

bullets hitting the fender drowned out the

phone. Mark managed to hit the windshield

of the Range Rover as he winced in pain. It

slowed Akbar's men down as one of the men

kicked the windshield out for visibility.

Sunni pushed the rental harder, quickly

approaching the consulate. They zoomed within its borders and Sunni slammed on brakes. She could hear the ambassador barking instructions for them to quickly come into the consulate borders. Mark instinctively dove across the seat and snatched up Brianna. Sunni grabbed the gun to cover Mark as he kicked open the door.

Adrenaline took over as Mark advanced to the consulate. Sunni showered bullets at the men approaching. The men were ordered by the ambassador to cease fire, or they would be killed. His blowhorn fell on death ears because they continued to advance and fire

their weapons. The officers fired on Akbar's

men and the SUV came to a screeching halt.

Sunni ran into the secure borders of the

consulate. Her adrenaline was high as she

ran to check on Brianna and Mark. Medical

staff frantically worked to stabilize Mark's

wounds. Sunni checked on Brianna while

Mark was being triaged. Medical staff

checked Brianna's vitals. She was conscious

but still somewhat disoriented. The doctor

asked if Sunni required medical attention

because her friends were ready to be

transported to the hospital. Sunni replied

that physically she was fine. Sunni talked

with Mark as they were taken to the

chopper. "It's gonna be alright guys.

Hang in there, we will be home before you

know it," Sunni assured them. "Home???

What about our cruise... incredibly Brianna

asked. Sunni began to laugh uncontrollably.

" A'nt that some shit? We damn near got

our ass shot off saving her and she don't

even know," Sunni joked. "Well, I know one

thing, me and my baby gonna work things

out." Mark said confidently. "Excuse me!"

Sunni interjected ceasing her laughter. You said that your boyfriend was shot. "That would be me," Mark said smiling. Before Sunni could respond, medical staff lifted Mark and Brianna in the chopper for transport. "I'll meet you soon," Sunni yelled as they flew off to the hospital.

Sunni had unfinished business. When Sunni arrived at the hospital, she went to see hospital administrators. Sunni wanted to make arrangements for Maria's remains. Sunni had won a lot of money in Mexico. That was the least she could do for Maria. Maria had been a true soldier. Sunni completed arrangements for Maria's burial and went to check on her friends. Brianna was coming along nicely. She was coherent and recognized her. Brianna hugged her friend. "You never gave up looking for me," Brianna cried. Sunni was crying too. This had been a terrible ordeal and they were overcome with emotion. Sunni reassured Brianna that they would be going home soon but she needed to check on Mark. The doctor was in Mark's room examining his wound. He had emergency surgery to close the wound. Luckily, the bullet went clean through so Mark did not require a transfusion. The doctor was checking his sutures as the nurse checked Mark's vitals. Mark was awake and asking questions. He wanted to know if his leg would heal fully. The doctor told Mark that if he wanted to get back on the football field, he had better follow medical instructions.

"Ok doc, I will. So, when can I get out of here?", Mark asked. "There you go being pushy, "Sunni joked." She knew Mark well enough to know that although he displayed a tough bravado, he was worried about his leg. If it did not heal properly, it could end his career. "I will sign discharge papers tomorrow provided you follow to my

instructions., agreed?", suggested the

doctor. "Yeah, sure doc," Mark replied. The

doctor left to attend the next patient. But

not before they thank him for his care.

"Mark, I need to talk to you for a minute. I

have something that I need to take care. I

brought yours and Bri's passports.

I'll leave the bags too. I know you are hurt

but I have faith that you will get Bri back

home. I'll meet you as soon as I can, ok?",

Sunni asked. Mark looked at her with

bewilderment. "We've just went through

hell...what are you doing?", Mark demanded to know.

"No worries, I'll be fine. I...I mean we got to this point, right? Before you know it, we'll be back home getting on each other's nerves again." Sunni smiled. She kissed Mark on his head and placed his passport in his hand.

Mark closed his eyes, savored her warm kiss, and wondered if he would see Sunni again.

Sunni was mentally and physically exhausted. But there was something that she had to do. Sunni went to the rental knowing that she had to book a flight to Mexico. She was headed back to Club 22.

On the way Sunni called the ambassador. He was glad to hear from her. "How are you and your friends?', he inquired. "The doctor said that they can travel soon, so, I'll make arrangements for flights home, Sunni informed him. "I thought that you would want to know that Johnson was taken into custody. The women that you and your friend saved are going to be alright," Ambassador Charles reassured her. Sunni blew a sigh of relief. "Maria's death has not been in vain. I made arrangements for her burial and a headstone with a little wind fall that I came into. I didn't have any information about her family", she told

Ambassador Charles. "I'll use my resources

to find any information that I can about

Maria family. Also, I can provide an escort

for you and your friends to ensure you get

on the plane safely. Unfortunately, we have

not received any word on the ringleader,"

Ambassador Charles warned.

"I can't tell you how thankful we are for all

the help that you have given us. You helped

save our lives," Sunni said fighting back

tears. "It has been a pleasure to serve you

Sunni. Thank you for helping to bring

criminals to justice. You saved innocent

women from sex exploitation. That was quite heroic. Thanks again. I want you to text me the details of your flight so, I can provide your escort. Feel free to call me when you get back home to let me know how everything is going, alright. You can call me anytime you need to, understood?", the ambassador asked. "Yes, I certainly will. Thank you so very much". Sunni ended the call. Sunni neglected to tell the ambassador

that she was about to book a flight to Mexico. She knew that he would probably try to dissuade her from going. She was nervous even terrified, but Sunni felt that

she had to go back.to the

The Confrontation

Sunni walked into the club and headed to the

casino bank. Sunni showed her identification

and requested her money. The banker

hesitated. "Is there a problem?" Sunny

sternly asked. "Just one moment," he

replied and picked up the phone to make a

call. Before she could blink Carlito was

standing there.

"So, we meet again, my sweet Sunni. You are

very resourceful, and you have grande las

pelotas. You have cause me much money.

Now what shall I do with you?" Carlito asked

rhetorically.

"Nada! I am recording you, right now and if

you touch me, I'll scream bloody murder

You will give me my money and watched me

walk out of this joint. I have friends in high

places. As a matter of fact. I have only to

push speed dial and a shit storm will fall

upon this club." Sunni looked at Carlito defiantly.

Carlito looked at Sunni. 'You think you are the only one with powerful friends? You better watch your back." Carlito said in a threatening manner. He nodded for the banker to pay Sunni her money. Sunni took her money and deliberately moved to the exit. She dared not look back. But, headed towards the airport. She couldn't believe that Carlito would let her go so easily. Sunni could not help but wonder what Carlito meant when he said that he knew people in high places too. She found a bank in the airport to wire most of the money to her account. She would take the rest and get a

a first-class ticket home. Something did not sit right with her conversation with Carlito. Sunni looked around expecting some goons to whisk her away at any moment.

"Looking for someone?" a familiar voice said. Sunni looked behind her and there was Mark and Bri smiling. She looked around at them two both sitting in wheelchairs. Sunni was never so glad to see two people in her life, but she played it off. "Well if this ain't two broke down.... . I'm so happy to see you guys", laughing as she hugged her friends. Sunni kissed them both. "See, I told you, you still loved me," Mark picked with Sunni. "Shut-up, man! What are you guys doing in Mexico?" Sunni inquired." "Lay over. We were just about to board. You get your unfinished business straight?" Mark asked. "Yes, I believe so, Let go home!" Sunni said emphatically. "Yea, this is the worst vacation ever...I need a drink!" Bri joked. "Really, bitch. I see you are back. A drink is what got us into trouble!" Sunni joked. They laughed heartily for as they boarded the plane for destination...home.   The End?

The characters and events are fictitious,

but sex trafficking is real.

Sex trafficking is a horrific crime. Women,

children, transgender and even men are

victims of this crime.

Human Trafficking Awareness

Hotline: 1-888-373-7888

Text: 233733

24/7 Confidential

Written: By **D C Bryant**

Thank You for reading look for a part two

soon!!!

Special thanks to my loving and supportive family. Thanks so much to Elaine for the gift!

My Cover Is By Nicole Watts

Website:

https://www.kreationsk.com/

Made in the USA
Middletown, DE
29 September 2021

48528210R00106